D1420640

You do not need to read this page - just get on with the book!

First published in Great Britain by Barrington Stoke Ltd
10 Belford Terrace, Edinburgh EH4 3DQ
Copyright © 2002 Douglas Hill
Illustrations © Tony Ross
The moral right of the author has been asserted in
accordance with the Copyright, Designs and
Patents Act 1988
ISBN 1-84299-046-2
Printed by Polestar AUP Aberdeen Ltd

MEET THE AUTHOR – DOUGLAS HILL

What is your favourite animal?
Cats - any and all
What is your favourite boy's name?
Michael - my son's name
What is your favourite girl's name?
Lauren
What is your favourite food?
Chocolate
What is your favourite music?
Mozart
What is your favourite hobby?
Reading

MEET THE ILLUSTRATOR – TONY ROSS

What is your favourite animal?
Cat
What is your favourite boy's name?
Bill
What is your favourite girl's name?
Roxanne
What is your favourite food?
Lobster
What is your favourite music?
Irish
What is your favourite hobby?
Sailing

Just for Rose
a star, not a dragon

Contents

1   World of Flame   1

2   Distant Mysteries   7

3   Grassland Planet   11

4   Strange Welcome   17

5   Terror from Space   23

6   Face of the Dragon   29

7   Doomed   35

8   A Slender Chance   39

9   Dangerous Chase   45

10 Mirry's Plan   49

11 Magical Image   53

12 Dragon's Fate   59

Chapter 1
World of Flame

Perrin and Mirry, on their starship, were looking at a small planet, spinning around a red sun. There was something odd about the planet. It was covered all over with a deep layer of cloud.

"It looks fluffy, as if it was wrapped in cotton wool," Perrin said.

He peered out of the window-port in the starship's control room. His friend Mirry, who was flying the ship, was watching the screen of the close-scanner as they got closer to the planet.

"The cloud layer is very deep," Mirry said. "And below it, the air is very thin and full of poisonous gases. So there is no life there."

"Another dead planet," Perrin sighed.

"Life is rare in the universe," Mirry reminded him.

She touched the controls, and the starship plunged down into the cloud. When it burst out into the open again, beneath the cloud layer, Perrin gasped.

The whole surface of the planet seemed to be on fire. Everywhere, giant volcanoes spouted flames into the air, with blasts of blazing ash and molten rock. On the ground, seas of red-hot lava boiled and flared. And all of it gave off huge drifts of smoke, which billowed up to join the cloud layer.

"That explains why there is no life," Mirry said.

Perrin frowned. "We'd better find a good planet soon," he muttered. "Or I'll be out of a job."

Perrin was a young man, not very tall, with brown hair and a boyish face. He and Mirry were planet-finders. Their job was to look for new planets with lots of interesting alien life. But though they had searched and searched among the stars for a month or more, they had found only one planet with any kind of life.

Perrin was afraid that if he didn't find a planet with life on it, quite soon, he would lose his job. And he really liked being a planet-finder – because he liked a quiet life. He was happy to drift around in space with nothing much to do except watch TV, read books, play computer games or gaze at the stars.

It was his friend Mirry who did most of the work on the starship. She was a very clever super-robot, who had been made for planet-finding.

The name of the company that made her was MIRI, and those letters were printed on her shoulder. Perrin had thought it sounded like a girl's name, so he called her Mirry and thought of her as a girl robot.

At the controls, Mirry took the ship back up, through the cloud layer. When they were in deep space again, she switched on the ship's far-scanner, which could gaze across enormous distances. And then she went quite still.

"Perrin, look," she said. "There is something impossible out there."

Chapter 2
Distant Mysteries

Perrin peered at the far-scanner's screen. It showed a bright object that was moving through space, a long, long way away from the ship.

But the object wasn't a comet or a meteor. It looked like a flying creature, with wide-swept wings. And it had to be incredibly huge, to be seen at such a distance.

"Whatever is that?" Perrin asked.

"I cannot tell," Mirry said. "It is acting as if it was alive. It keeps changing direction. As if it was searching for something."

"How can it be alive, out in empty space?" Perrin asked.

"We might find out," Mirry said, "if we get closer."

"Fine," Perrin said. "Let me know when we're there."

He headed for the door. Before they found the fiery planet, he had been watching an exciting TV film about Earth's olden days, with knights fighting monsters. He wanted to get back to it.

But as he reached the control-room door, Mirry called, "Wait, Perrin!"

Perrin turned with a frown. "What now?"

"I turned the far-scanner round, to look at another part of space," Mirry announced, "and I spotted something else!"

Perrin went back to the far-scanner screen, where he saw a bright point of light, with an even smaller speck of light beside it.

"A distant star," Mirry said, "with a planet!"

Perrin smiled happily. "This is quite a day. We've found a dead, fiery planet, a weird flying creature, and now another planet! I hope this one is some good."

"Let us go and see," Mirry said. "We can come back later, to look at that flying thing."

And the starship flashed away, towards the unknown world.

Chapter 3
Grassland Planet

It was a long way to the planet, so the starship needed a day or two to reach it. Perrin was able to watch several films. But he also spent some time every day with Mirry, in the control room.

One day, while he was with her, a loud chime sounded. On another screen, the stern face of a man appeared.

That screen was on a space-link that connected them to Earth. The face belonged to Commander Cragg, boss of the Planet-Finding Project.

"Anything to report, Perrin?" Cragg snapped. "Or are you having a holiday?"

"As a matter of fact, we're going to look at a planet right now," Perrin said stiffly.

Cragg sniffed. "Probably another of your dead ones," he snarled. "Give me a report as soon as possible." And the screen went blank.

"I wish he'd leave us alone!" Perrin fumed.

"Do not let him upset you," Mirry said. "We have found a planet to look at."

When they were close enough to see the new planet clearly, they saw, to their delight, that it was far from dead. Its largest piece of land was an enormous plain of lush, yellow-green grass, fed by bright rivers.

As Mirry set the ship down on to the plain, they saw two things speeding over the grass. Big, round, silvery things, like huge upside-down bathtubs.

"Alien beings!" Mirry said.

Perrin looked worried. "They're very big. And they're coming this way."

"Put on your space-suit, Perrin," Mirry said. "The air here is unfit for humans."

Perrin slowly pulled on his space-suit. The Planet-Finding Project insisted that a human – which meant Perrin – should be the first to meet any intelligent aliens. That was so the aliens would know that Earth people were humans, not robots like Mirry.

But Perrin was not keen to go out and face strange creatures he knew nothing about.

Still, his light but tough space-suit would protect him. And so would Mirry, whose metal body was incredibly strong.

He trudged glumly to the airlock that led out of the ship. "Stay awake, Mirry," he said.

"Robots are always awake," Mirry said.

The airlock opened, and Perrin stepped out on to the landing ramp. He flinched as the airlock closed behind him, then stared at the two huge, tub-shaped things moving towards him.

They were the size of large trucks on Earth, with wide, soft wheels. And that seemed odd. Perrin had never heard of alien beings who had wheels instead of legs.

But then, on the side of each big, round tub, doors opened. And Perrin realised that the round things weren't the aliens. They were just for transport.

Through the open doors, the real aliens poured out.

Chapter 4
Strange Welcome

They all had blue skins, hairless heads and round, pale eyes, and all wore short, baggy robes. And they streamed towards the ship, shouting.

Perrin drew back. "Mirry!" he hissed, over his helmet's voice-link. "Let me back in!"

But the airlock stayed shut. And the aliens kept coming. "Hurry, Mirry!" Perrin shouted.

Still the airlock didn't open. And the aliens had nearly reached the ramp.

"*Mirry*!" Perrin yelled. "Stop being absent-minded!"

It was something that Mirry did, now and then. Often at the worst possible time. It seemed as if she forgot what was happening around her, and drifted off somewhere else in her mind. But she would never admit it.

"I am *not* absent-minded," Mirry's voice said in his helmet ear-piece. "I was studying the aliens – and I believe they mean no harm. Look at them."

The crowd of aliens had stopped at the foot of the landing ramp. And they were gazing at Perrin with what looked like joy.

One of them, probably a leader, stepped forward. "*Muzzzz frilliji*!" it said.

Perrin switched on his Word-Wizard. It was a tiny super-computer, in his helmet, that could learn a whole alien language from hearing only a few words.

"*Wheeffel ...*" said the alien. And then the Word-Wizard in Perrin's helmet began to translate. "Welcome to our world," the alien was saying, "which we call Elashel. Are you the great one who will save us?"

"What do you mean, save you?" Perrin said. At once the Word-Wizard translated his words, too, so the aliens heard their own language from his helmet speaker.

The aliens looked thrilled. "He speaks our language!" the first alien said to the others. "This must indeed be the mighty one, come from the sky to save our world!"

"Hang on," Perrin said. "What's all this saving stuff?"

"You have come just in time, great one," the alien leader said. "The monster has returned, as the prophecy said it would. And its path will lead it *here* – to attack us!"

Perrin gulped. "Monster?" he echoed.

"The Sacred Stones of our forefathers tell of it," the alien said. "It is a winged monster of enormous size. It came from space more than a thousand years ago and it brought terror and ruin to our lands ... Even worse, it swallowed up much of our world's *water*, which was nearly the end of us."

"That's ... terrible," Perrin whispered.

"And now," the alien leader went on, "as the Stones foretold, the monster is returning – to threaten Elashel again. Our telescopes have seen it, far away among the stars. Just as they saw your approach, mighty one, which the Sacred Stones also foretold. A hero from the sky, arriving to save us from the monster."

Chapter 5
Terror from Space

Perrin was astonished. "I'm no hero. I'm just Perrin. I'm just an ordinary human."

"A being who soars among the stars in a great machine," the alien said, "must be a hero. So we welcome you, Lord Perrin. I am Lynnia, High Mother of Elashel. If you will come with us to our Great Hall, you may see the monster for yourself."

"All right," Perrin said. "But I'll want to bring my friend."

He introduced them to Mirry, who amazed them even more. "A wonderful flying machine, and a friend who is also a machine!" Lynnia cried. "Truly you are the great one, Lord Perrin!"

Then they all climbed into the big, round transporters and rolled away across the plain.

Before long they came to a cluster of stone buildings, which turned out to be the main city. And the city's biggest building was the Great Hall.

There Perrin found that being an important visitor can be quite boring.

First, several of the blue-skinned aliens made long speeches of welcome. Then Perrin was shown the Sacred Stones – huge, flat slabs with masses of tiny words carved on them – where the aliens chanted long prayers.

After that, they all sat down to a feast. But Perrin couldn't eat anything because he had to keep his helmet on to breathe and Mirry didn't eat anything because robots don't eat. Then there were even more speeches.

Finally, Lynnia and the others took them to the topmost part of the Hall, where giant telescopes gazed at the clear night sky, brilliant with stars.

And there Perrin stopped feeling bored, as he saw the terror that the planet faced.

In one part of the sky, a weird shape could be seen. It was like a black outline that covered some of the stars.

A shape like a flying creature, with wide, arched wings.

"See, Lord Perrin," Lynnia said. "It sweeps through the emptiness like a bird of prey, seeking worlds to destroy."

"I think we saw it, in space, earlier," Perrin said.

"Quite so," Mirry agreed, as she peered through another telescope. "That is the winged creature we saw, far away, when we were leaving the fiery planet."

"Then you know how enormous it is," Lynnia said. "And it flies as swiftly as a comet – so it may be upon us in no more than a week." She gazed at Perrin hopefully. "But I expect you have a plan to deal with it."

"Well, I ... I ..." Perrin gulped.

"*Lord* Perrin," Mirry said brightly, "will wish to go back into space first, for a closer look at the creature."

"I'd like to go back into space and keep on going," Perrin muttered, on the voice-link that only Mirry could hear.

The aliens looked delighted. "As it is written on the Stones," Lynnia cried, "we will be saved!"

Chapter 6
Face of the Dragon

Later, back in the starship, Perrin was not happy. "What am I going to do, Mirry?" he moaned. "These aliens expect me to act like a great hero!"

"You would be a hero," Mirry said, "if we were able to save them."

Perrin blinked. "How could we save them?"

"If we take a closer look at the monster," Mirry said, "we might have some ideas."

So they blasted away into space. The journey took some time, since the monster was still a great distance from the aliens' planet, Elashel. But at last Perrin and Mirry were close enough to see the creature more clearly.

And it was terrifying.

It was bigger than the biggest mountain on Earth. In fact it was the most enormous living thing that Perrin had ever seen.

"It is not a giant bird," Mirry said. "Instead of a beak, this creature has strange, long jaws."

Weird, Perrin thought. It's like the dragon-monster in that TV film with the knights. Only a lot bigger.

A star dragon ...

They also realised, as they drew nearer, that the monster seemed to be made entirely of *ice*. Like a gigantic, frozen statue, which was somehow alive.

Its ice-body was thick and solid, with a long, snaky neck, and it was covered with massive scales that were overlapping layers of ice, each as thick as a glacier.

But its head was the worst of all. The eyes were like vast, blank, icy caves, while the dragon-jaws were filled with glittering fangs like giant icicles.

Perrin shivered. "Let's not get too close," he muttered.

But the starship went rushing on, at full speed.

"Mirry?" Perrin said. "Shouldn't we slow down?"

But Mirry sat quite still, and her eyes looked faintly dim as if her mind had begun to drift off.

Then the star dragon's terrible head started to swing towards the ship and its vast body began to turn.

"Mirry!" Perrin gasped. "It's seen us!"

Still Mirry didn't move. The ship hurtled on. By then, the monster had fully turned and was looming towards them, its fanged mouth open.

"*Mirry!*" Perrin howled. "Get us out of here!"

"Mm?" said Mirry absently. "Oh, yes." And just in time she swung the ship away.

But still the dragon stormed after them, with its mouth gaping hungrily.

"It's chasing us!" Perrin cried.

"There is no danger," Mirry said. "Our starship is much faster."

She touched a control, and the ship shot away, far out of reach.

Perrin took a deep, shaky breath. "One day," he told Mirry, "you'll go absent-minded and get us killed."

"I was *not* being absent-minded," Mirry said firmly. "I was scanning the creature. Within its great ice-body, there are strange forces that give it life. It must take in water, from the planets it attacks, to build up its ice. Most strange."

"And scary," Perrin muttered.

"Quite so," Mirry said. "Those aliens would be helpless against such a monster."

Chapter 7
Doomed

"We'd better go and tell them that we can't help them," Perrin said sadly.

"But it will not reach their world for many days," Mirry said. "We have time to think of something."

"We need a miracle," Perrin grumbled.

"We must try," Mirry insisted. "We cannot just turn away."

"Try what?" Perrin asked. "We don't have any weapons. We don't have *anything* that would stop something the size of the star dragon."

"Star dragon ..." Mirry repeated. "What a good name for it."

"But no knight could defeat this dragon," Perrin muttered. "Too bad the aliens don't have spaceships, so they could escape."

"They have not yet even invented aircraft," Mirry replied. "No, Perrin, if anything is to be done, it will have to be done by us."

Perrin frowned. Then he jumped – when the chime of the space-link with Earth rang out again.

On the screen, Commander Cragg was scowling. "Perrin!" he barked. "Where's your report on that new planet?"

"I ... I was just ..." Perrin stammered.

Cragg sneered. "It's another dead, useless one, isn't it?"

"No, Commander," Mirry said before Perrin could reply. "It is an excellent planet, with friendly aliens. But it is also in grave danger." And she explained about the star dragon, and the threat to Elashel.

Cragg scowled again. "If that planet is going to be attacked, you'd better forget about it and start looking for others."

"Not yet," Mirry said firmly. And she went on – though Perrin tried to stop her – to tell Cragg that the aliens believed that

Perrin was a great hero who would save their world.

"Perrin? A hero?" Cragg roared with laughter. "What a joke! If those aliens are depending on Perrin to save them, they're doomed!"

Chapter 8
A Slender Chance

"You didn't need to tell him all that hero stuff," Perrin grumbled, after Cragg had switched off. "It just gave him another chance to be nasty."

"Never mind," Mirry said. "It is the fate of these aliens that is important."

Perrin sighed. "I wish I really were a hero," he muttered. "So I *could* save them."

"We are only what we are," Mirry said.

Perrin was silent and gloomy all the way back to Elashel. And when Lynnia and a crowd of aliens arrived at the ship as before, he felt even gloomier. They were all so hopeful that he had found some way to save their world.

"We ... we haven't exactly worked out what to do, yet," he told Lynnia.

Lynnia looked worried. "Time is short, Lord Perrin. The monster will be upon us in a matter of days."

"I know," Perrin mumbled. "But it's hard to see how to stop something so big."

"Perhaps," Lynnia said, "instead of trying to stop the monster, you and your flying machine might be able to *divert* it."

"Divert?" Perrin said, frowning.

"Make it turn aside, on a new course, so it misses this planet," Mirry said.

"How?" Perrin asked. "Push it away with the starship? It'd be like throwing a pebble at a mountain. It's already tried to eat us, when we got too close to it!"

Lynnia looked crushed. "I'm so sorry, Lord Perrin," she said. "I had no idea."

"Still," Mirry murmured, "it is a useful line of thought."

"Then go ahead and think," Perrin said crossly. "But all this worry is giving me a headache, and I'm going to have a rest." Perrin marched up the landing ramp, back into the ship.

Some time later, after a refreshing nap, he was feeling less grumpy. He was also watching another TV film – about pirates in the olden days on Earth – when Mirry came to find him.

"Perrin," she said, "I believe I have found a possible solution."

Perrin froze the image on the screen – a wide view of an ocean with white-crested waves. "A way to stop the star dragon?"

"To turn it aside," Mirry said. "We could use the starship as bait – to make the dragon chase us, as it did before. So we could draw it away from this world."

"I don't know ..." Perrin muttered.

"Remember that our ship is much faster," Mirry said. "We can easily stay out of the dragon's reach."

Perrin sighed, then shrugged. "I suppose we could give it a try."

Shortly afterwards the starship lifted off, to seek the star dragon again.

Chapter 9
Dangerous Chase

By then, the dragon was much closer to Elashel – still flying on, tireless and terrible.

Perrin stared from the window-port at the monstrous, icy shape. "Mirry," he said, "when the dragon starts chasing us, *please* don't go absent-minded."

"I do not go absent-minded," Mirry insisted. "I only ... pause for thought."

"If you pause out here," Perrin told her, "the dragon will have us for lunch." He sighed. "If only I could fly the starship ..."

"You would need years of training," Mirry said, "and the help of a super-computer. Whereas my brain *is* such a computer, with the training programmed in."

"I know, I know," Perrin grumbled. Then they fell silent – for they were once again close to the star dragon's terrible face.

And when the monster spotted the ship, it turned towards it, as it had done before.

Perrin turned cold as he watched the frightful jaws open, to show the huge ice-fangs. But at least Mirry's eyes weren't dim, as in her absent-minded times.

At the very last minute, with the dragon's fangs almost upon them, Mirry sent the starship flashing away. Then she slowed it again.

As they hoped, the dragon came after them. So Mirry did it again, and again ...

The plan worked perfectly. The dragon kept chasing the ship, on and on. After more than an hour, it was actually farther away from Elashel than it had been when Perrin and Mirry first saw it.

Also, by then, they had turned the dragon around. It was now flying in the opposite direction, *away* from Elashel – getting farther away every moment.

"Isn't this far enough?" Perrin said. "Can't we leave it to fly off by itself?"

"Probably," Mirry agreed.

She touched a control, and the ship shot away. In seconds it had left the monster far behind.

"Brilliant," Perrin said with a grin. "The aliens will be thrilled..."

Then they both went quiet.

They were watching the star dragon's distant shape on the far-scanner screen. As they watched, the dragon began to turn.

Steadily it came around, till it was on the same course as before.

Heading back towards Elashel.

Chapter 10
Mirry's Plan

"So much for that idea," Perrin muttered.

"At least we have gained time," Mirry said. "It will take the dragon nearly two more weeks, now, to reach Elashel. By then we may have thought of something."

Perrin sighed – then blinked at the far-scanner. On its screen he could see something familiar, far beyond the winged shape of the dragon.

"I wish," he said, "the dragon would go and attack that planet with the volcanoes, the one we saw before." He pointed at the scanner screen, which showed a speck of light that was the distant fiery planet. "The dragon would melt."

Mirry stared at him. "What a very good idea!"

Perrin frowned. "I wasn't being serious."

"Perhaps not," Mirry replied. "But still ..."

On another screen, she brought up a photo of the fiery planet that she had taken when they had first spotted it. They gazed at that small world, under its covering of pale cloud – which gave no hint of the flaming volcanoes and boiling lava, below.

"The monster would not know that there is fire on the planet, below the cloud," Mirry said. "If we could lure it there ..."

"But the cloud screen might put it off," Perrin said. "Anyway, it only attacks planets like Elashel, because it needs water."

Mirry twitched. "That is it, Perrin!" she cried. "That is the way to lure it!"

She sent the starship blasting away towards the fiery planet, ignoring Perrin's startled questions. Then she put the ship on auto-pilot, and rushed off.

For some time she was hard at work. Sometimes she was busy with strange calculations, at other times she seemed to be building something. And when they finally reached the fiery planet, she spent a while on the outside of the ship, doing more puzzling things.

Perrin found all the mystery very annoying. And he was even more annoyed when his TV stopped working, and Mirry was too busy to fix it.

But at last she had finished. And then she took the ship away from the fiery planet.

Back towards the distant star dragon.

"Are you going to tell me what's going on?" Perrin grumbled.

"I will soon be able to show you," Mirry said brightly.

And she said nothing more, as the starship hurtled on.

Chapter 11
Magical Image

At last they caught up with the dragon, as it flew steadily on towards Elashel. And once again Mirry took the ship near its face, inviting it to chase them.

But this time the dragon ignored the ship and flew straight on towards Elashel.

"It has clearly learned from before," Mirry said, "that we are hard to catch. We must *make* it chase us."

She sent the ship shooting forward – towards the huge, dark pit that was one of the monster's eyes.

Perrin looked worried. "You're not going to fly in there, are you?" he asked.

"No," Mirry said. "Wait."

The ship blasted on. The dragon still ignored it. Then at the last moment, Mirry swung the ship around and away, in a sharp swerve. That caused the white-hot flame of its engines to sweep across the dragon's eye.

In the heat of that flame, part of the icy ridge of the eye-socket melted. It froze again, at once, in the total cold of outer space. But the brief melting had either hurt the dragon, or made it angry. In any case, it worked.

The monster swung its head and snapped with giant fangs at the speeding starship.

And then it came charging after them.

"Here we go!" Perrin cried.

As before, Mirry carefully kept the ship just out of reach, as she led the raging monster all the way back to the fiery planet. And when they arrived, high above the planet's layer of cloud, Mirry touched a switch.

Perrin gasped in amazement.

It was like magic. In place of the pale sweep of cloud over the planet, Perrin saw a great expanse of blue ocean, with white-crested waves.

"You gave me the idea, Perrin," Mirry said brightly. "You called it a cloud screen – and you reminded me that the dragon seeks water. You are seeing an image of an ocean, taken from your TV film about pirates. I have greatly enlarged it and projected it onto the cloud, as a film is projected onto a screen."

"How?" Perrin breathed.

"I used your TV system," Mirry told him, "and gave it extra power from the ship's engines. The dragon, I hope, will think that it is a real ocean. And now we must try to make it rush down to the planet at great speed."

"So that's what happened to my TV," Perrin muttered. Then he jumped, as Mirry sent the ship into a dive towards the planet.

And the star dragon plunged after them, towards what it thought was a deep, inviting ocean.

All at once the starship stopped, to hover just above the cloud. But the dragon kept coming, faster and faster, as if it was desperate to get at the water. And it was coming straight down, directly at the ship.

"It's getting close, Mirry," Perrin said. "Let's move!"

Mirry said nothing, and her eyes had gone dim.

"Mirry!" Perrin cried. "The dragon's coming right down on top of us!"

Still Mirry did not speak or move.

And the monster thundered down upon them, almost blotting out the sky.

Chapter 12
Dragon's Fate

"*Mirry!*" Perrin yelled.

"Mm?" Mirry said absently. "Oh, yes."

But the ship didn't move to one side, out of danger. To Perrin's horror, it dived straight down *into* the cloud.

With the dragon still storming down above them ... on top of them.

"Before you say anything," Mirry said calmly, "I was *not* being absent-minded. We had to stay there, to project the image of the ocean right up to the last minute."

"Mirry!" Perrin yelled wildly. "The *dragon* ...!"

"Wait," she said.

The starship burst out of the cloud, and swooped down towards the fiery surface of the planet. Then at last it swerved to one side, where it stopped and hovered again.

Perrin and Mirry sat and watched, in silent amazement.

When the dragon hit the cloud layer, it must have known at once that there was no ocean. But it was too huge and was moving too fast, and the planet's surface was too close. It couldn't stop.

Its enormous icy mass plunged down out
of the cloud – missing the starship – and
crashed into the seething ocean of lava.

Before its wings could start to heave its
vast weight into the air again, the red-hot
lava did its work.

In that deadly heat, the dragon's wings drooped, its jaws dripped and the whole colossal body grew smaller and smaller.

At last, like an ice cube in hot water, the star dragon melted away, and vanished.

For a long, silent time, Perrin and Mirry stared at the ocean of lava – where nothing stirred except flickering flames.

"It's gone," Perrin whispered at last. "You did it, Mirry!"

"*We* did it, Perrin," Mirry said. "It was your idea, remember, to lure the dragon to the fiery world."

Perrin shook his head. "That was just a wish. I didn't think it was possible ..." He grinned. "But the prophecy on the aliens' Sacred Stones has come true!"

"And you can tell Commander Cragg that you are a hero after all," Mirry said.

"He'll never believe me," Perrin muttered. Then he peered down at the lava again. "Do you think the dragon is really dead?"

"The strange forces that gave it life may still be alive, down there," Mirry said. "But it will not be able to make another body of ice from the depths of a fiery sea."

"Then let's go tell the aliens they're safe," Perrin said happily.

Mirry sent the ship flashing back into deep space, towards Elashel. "I expect," she said, "they will have another feast to celebrate your victory."

Perrin looked delighted – until he thought of something, and groaned. "So there'll be more long, boring speeches."

"Of course," Mirry agreed. "Heroes have to put up with speeches."

"Then let's make sure," Perrin said, "that the *next* planet we find doesn't need to be saved from anything."

Barrington Stoke was a famous and much-loved story-teller. He travelled from village to village carrying a lantern to light his way. He arrived as it grew dark and when the young boys and girls of the village saw the glow of his lantern, they hurried to the central meeting place. They were full of excitement and expectation, for his stories were always wonderful.

Then Barrington Stoke set down his lantern. In the flickering light the listeners were enthralled by his tales of adventure, horror and mystery. He knew exactly what they liked best and he loved telling a good story. And another. And then another. When the lantern burned low and dawn was nearly breaking, he slipped away. He was gone by morning, only to appear the next day in some other village to tell the next story.

Barrington Stoke would like to thank all its readers for commenting on the manuscript before publication and in particular:

David Asquith
Adam Asquith
Hugh Barnard
Bobby Burns
Danielle Collister
Ashley Cottrell
Susan Cranfield
Luke Ellingworth
J Gripper
Lewis Hind
Moira Kleissner

Callum Marshall
Christopher Moody
Sean Povey
Sheila Raftery
Daniel Reid
Angus Reynolds
Sam Skelt
Tom Slater
Amy Stewart
Alastair Train

Barrington Stoke Club

Would you like to become a member of our club? Children who write to us with their views become members of our club and special advisors to the company. They also have the chance to act as editors on future manuscripts. Contact us at the address or website below – we'd love to hear from you!

Barrington Stoke, 10 Belford Terrace, Edinburgh EH4 3DQ
Tel: 0131 315 4933 Fax: 0131 315 4934
E-mail: info@barringtonstoke.co.uk
Website: www.barringtonstoke.co.uk

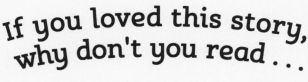

If you loved this story, why don't you read ...

Monster Maze

by Douglas Hill

Have you ever had to make a quick getaway? Perrin is exploring a new planet with his robot friend Mirry. But when a cliff collapses and falls on top of her, he has to act fast. He is lost and all alone. Find out what happens as Perrin and Mirry discover the terror that lies at the heart of the monster maze.

You can order this book directly from:
Macmillan Distribution Ltd, Brunel Road, Houndmills,
Basingstoke, Hampshire RG21 6XS
Tel: 01256 302699